CTW

SESAME STREET®

Music Concepts

SOFT AND LOUD

featuring

BERT AND ERNIE

Story by: Dina Anastasio
Illustrations by: Tom Brannon
Publisher: Mr. Lauren Keiser
The audio was produced at
Wood Studios, Greenwich, CT

Early one morning, Ernie jumped out of bed and poked his good friend Bert.

"Hey Bert," Ernie said. "Did you hear that loud, loud noise?"

"What noise?" Bert said, rubbing his eyes. "I didn't hear anything."

"You must have heard it," Ernie said. "It was VERY, VERY loud. It was so loud that it woke me up."

"What did it sound like?" Bert asked.

"Hmmm," said Ernie. "I'll have to think about that."

3

Bert sat up and looked at the clock.

"Hey Ernie," he said. "It's seven o'clock. We're supposed to meet Big Bird in the park in a half an hour."

Ernie went to his closet and took out his clothes. While he was getting dressed, he hummed softly and thought about the loud sound.

When Ernie was ready, he followed Bert outside and looked up at the sky.

"Gee Bert," Ernie said. "Isn't it a nice day to go to the park?"

Bert and Ernie walked down Sesame Street. When they were almost to the corner, a little red bird flew over Ernie's head and sat on a branch nearby.

"Cheep, cheep, cheep," said the bird.

Bert stopped.

"Hold it, Ernie," he said. "Is that the sound that woke you up this morning?"

Ernie listened carefully. "Cheep, cheep, cheep," said the bird.

"That's a different sound," said Ernie. "That sound is much softer than the sound that woke me up."

Bert and Ernie said goodbye to the little red bird and walked on. As they were passing Mr. Hooper's store, they heard a loud, loud noise, and before long a fire engine whizzed by.

"Hey Ernie," Bert said. "I'll bet THAT'S the loud noise that woke you up."

"No, no," Ernie said. "It was a loud noise, Bert, but it wasn't THAT loud."

Bert and Ernie went on. After awhile they turned a corner and stopped.

"Listen Ernie," Bert said softly. "Do you hear that BOOM! BOOM! BOOM! sound?"

"I hear it," Ernie said. "It sure is loud. I wonder what it is."

"Maybe THAT'S the sound that woke you up," Bert said.
"No, no, no," Ernie said. "It wasn't a loud BOOM! BOOM! BOOM! sound."

Bert and Ernie waited. The BOOM! BOOM! BOOM! got louder and louder and louder.

All of a sudden the BOOM! BOOM! BOOM! turned the corner and came toward them.

"Look Bert!" Ernie cried. "The BOOM! BOOM! BOOM is a drum. And behind the BOOM! BOOM! BOOM! is a great big parade."

12

Bert and Ernie watched the parade for awhile and then they headed for the park.

Every time a car horn honked, Bert said, "Is that the sound that woke you up?"

And Ernie said, "That's a loud sound, Bert old buddy. But that's not the sound that woke me up."

And every time a little mouse or a little chipmunk or a little frog made a little sound, Ernie said, "Nope. That's a soft sound. THAT'S not the sound that woke me up."

Bert and Ernie were almost to the park when the sky grew dark and the wind began to blow softly. The leaves on the trees made a soft rustling sound.

"We'd better hurry," Ernie said. "We'd better find Big Bird before it begins to rain."

Bert and Ernie ran as fast as they could.

Bert and Ernie ran into the park. They looked by the sandbox.
They looked by the swings. They looked by the slide. Big Bird
wasn't there.

Bert and Ernie were walking past the baseball field when they heard a GREAT BIG LOUD BOOM.

"It's the drum!" Ernie cried.

Bert laughed. "That's not the drum," he said. "That's thunder, and we'd better get home before it starts to rain."

Bert and Ernie raced toward home. The sky grew darker and darker, and the rain began to fall.

The first drop was tiny and soft, and it landed right smack on the tip of Ernie's nose. The next drop landed on the top of Bert's head. It made a soft "plunk" sound.

"Is that the sound that woke you up?" Bert asked.

"No, no." Ernie said. "The sound that woke me up was much louder."

21

Bert and Ernie ran up the steps and opened their front door.
Ernie stopped and stood very still.

"Listen," he said. "That's IT!"

"That's what?" Bert asked.

"The sound! The sound that woke me up!"

Bert listened, and then he laughed.
"That's not a loud sound, Ernie," he said. "That's the telephone."
"It's loud when you're sleeping, old buddy," Ernie said.
Bert picked up the telephone. It was Big Bird calling.

When Bert was finished talking, he hung up the phone.

"Guess what, Ernie," Bert said. "That was Big Bird calling this morning. He called to tell us that it was going to rain. He didn't go to the park."

Ernie laughed softly. Then he laughed LOUDER and LOUDER and LOUDER, until he couldn't laugh any more.

24